To all childhood dogs
— L. B.

First Edition

Library of Congress Cataloging–in–Publication Data

Boyd, Lizi, 1953–
   Black dog/red house / by Lizi Boyd. — 1st ed.
       p.   cm.
   Summary: Black Dog and friend explore a world of color
inside and outside the Red House.
   ISBN 0-316-10443-4
   [1. Color – Fiction. 2. Dogs – Fiction.]   I. Title.
PZ7.B6924B1 1993
[E] – dc20   92-1408
                       10 9 8 7 6 5 4 3 2 1
                              EV
            Published simultaneously in Canada by
          Little, Brown & Company (Canada) Limited
                    Printed in Hong Kong

BLACK DOG RED HOUSE

BY LIZI BOYD

Little, Brown and Company

Boston Toronto London

Together we roam,
inside
and
out.

Black dog
watches
as I wash

with the pink

washcloth.

While I eat,
black dog waits

by my yellow

high chair.

Black dog
wags his tail
as I build with blocks

by the blue

couch.

Black dog

chases the ball

under the turquoise

chest.

I giggle.
Black dog barks.

Mama says, "Outside,"
as she opens the brown

door.

We run,
fall down,
and roll

in the green

grass.

We lie on our backs and watch the big

white clouds.

We step
on our
long

gray shadows.

Black dog

plays with me

under the orange

sun.

Then we go inside.
I take off

my magenta

cap.

I climb into bed.
Black dog jumps in, too.

I take off my purple

socks.

I pull up the quilt
of many colors

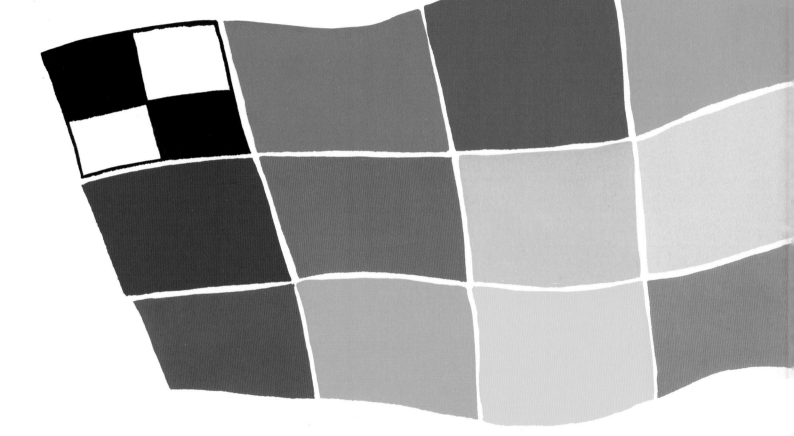

and together

we take a nap.